THE COLVERS REPORT

by Stephen L. Wynn

DORRANCE
PUBLISHING CO
EST. 1920
PITTSBURGH, PENNSYLVANIA 15238

Dorrance Publishing Co
585 Alpha Drive
Suite 103
Pittsburgh, PA 15238
Visit our website at *www.dorrancebookstore.com*

ISBN: 979-8-8852-7262-9
eISBN: 979-8-8852-7704-4

Special Acknowledgement

I would like to extend a huge thanks to Dorrance Publising Company, especially to their great support staff, who were always patient and understanding with my many calls of questions, they were all very professional and easy to work with, making this first time writing experience uncomplicated and enjoyable.

I also have a special thanks to Christine. She is someone I rely on immensely and who wears many hats. My personal assistant, my IT person, my proof reader and one who can point out my many errors without being offensive, to list just a few. Without her none of this would have been possible.

And to my non-human staff, My Google Home assistant, who is always available 24/7, always giving me valuable information, correct spelling and even telling me a funny joke or two when I ask.

Without any of them this book could not have been written.

Index

1973
From the author

What a year it was. My thoughts were to write a story on a major event from that year. There were many to choose from:

Richard M. Nixon is our 37th President of the United States, soon to be replaced by Gerald Ford.

Vietnam was coming to an end.

Secretariat wins the Triple Crown in thoroughbred racing.

Reggie Jackson leads the Oakland Athletics to victory over the New York Mets in the World Series.

The American Indian Movement had its seventy-one-day standoff with Federal authorities at the Pine Ridge Reservation in Wounded Knee South Dakota.

American space astronauts spent twenty-eight days in the first U.S. space station called Skylab.

The first handheld cellular phone call was made on April 3rd by Martin Cooper in New York City.

Federal Express officially begins operations on April 17th by launching fourteen small aircrafts from Memphis International Airport.

However, as interesting as all those events are...my curiosity was drawn to a sad article I found in the El Paso Texas Gazette of a double murder, and as harsh and disturbing as a double murder can be, the newspaper article tells how Howard Mitchel, a poor, uneducated black man was knowingly innocent but was still convicted and was executed for this double murder. The article goes on to say how the Department of Justice requested an investigation into this case.

I have chosen to write this book on the trials and tribulations of Mr. Howard Mitchell. Many judicial scholars, former judges, and law enforcement agents think this trial was the most unethical and illegitimate murder trial ever held in the State of Texas. Ryan Carter of the U.S. Marshals office brings you front and center with this gripping and compelling story with evidence he uncovered that shows Howard Mitchel was indeed an innocent man.

Chapter One
Wednesday, October 14th, 1993

"I'm innocent, you have the wrong man." Those were the last words spoken by Howard Mitchel before he was executed on May 12th, 1979.

My name is Ryan Carter, I'm with the U.S. Marshals office in El Paso, Texas. Fourteen years after his execution, the Department of Justice has directed me to reopen Howard Mitchel's murder case and look at the evidence that was presented at trial. You are about to read one week's worth of notes and conversations from my final report, now known as the Colvers Report, that I sent to the Department of Justice, Civil Rights Division.

Howard Mitchel was found guilty in the State of Texas and was executed for murdering John and Harriet Colver in Fort Stockton, Texas, but I will tell you right now the evidence that I found indeed shows Howard Mitchel was completely innocent and was not involved in any way with the murders of John and Harriet Colver. After reviewing old court documents, the evidence that was used to arrest and convict Howard was all circumstantial and very weak at best. Another part of my assignment was to investigate the mysterious deaths of six of the jurors from the Howard Mitchel's case, along with the brutal execution of the former lead prosecutor of the case, Vernon Birchmeyer. A lot of dead bodies and all with one connection...The Howard Mitchel case. As far as the six deceased jurors are concerned, they were not sweet, innocent people. Granted they didn't deserve to be murdered, but they were a big part in the injustice for Howard.

You will see and read new evidence that we uncovered, which allowed us to arrest the actual murderers of John and Harriet and solve the deaths of the six jurors. Evidence will show how Howard's trial was a complete scam. It took just weeks for the trial, where usually a double murder trial could take up to a year...

Hell, even the jurors were handpicked...you read that right...handpicked. Just about everyone in the courthouse at that time has Howard's blood on their hands. From the Judge, to the attorney, to law enforcement, all the way down to the county cook whose job was to feed the inmates did not provide justice to Howard. I wish I could tell Howard how I believe in him and how sorry I am. I can't imagine how scared he must have been as he was sitting in his jail cell. He was subjected to multiple beatings. He was fed one meal a day with food even a dog wouldn't eat. He was literally treated like an animal. From the moment he was arrested to the day of his execution, he was never allowed to see his wife or children. Through this investigation, myself and my team came to realize how hard and scary it had to of been to be black and live in rural Texas back then.

Howard's life story is like every other black man from that area...in that time. He came from a hardworking and very unlucky family. He had three older brothers and five sisters. When Howard was six-years-old, he was forced to watch...as his father was hung from the tree in their front yard and saw their house burnt to the ground.

His mother had to send his brothers and sisters to other families to live. Howard lived with and took care of his mother until she died when he was fourteen-years-old. Howard married Althea Jones when they were both sixteen-years-old. They had one son and two daughters. Howard and Althea both worked two jobs each to support their family. All three children graduated from high school. Howard had a third-grade education, he could not read or write. Althea has a sixth-grade education. Their one son, Byron, has served sixteen years in the Army and is now stationed in Germany. He is married with two children. One daughter is the head librarian at the El Paso County library after receiving her college degree from the University of Texas, and their other daughter is married and has three children and lives in Atlanta, Georgia.

Howard's family now knows the truth that their father, grandfather, and husband did not commit murder. I have shown that he was a victim of the highest level of racism and that he truly was good and honest and a great family man. After I met this family, I was amazed how they handled the pain and hardships life has given them. Never asking for any handouts or seeking any revenge. The local Baptist church did hold a fundraiser though and raised enough money to build a two-bedroom home for Althea.

This nightmare started on Tuesday, April 18th, 1973 at 8:05 P.M. when an anonymous phone call came into the El Paso County Sheriff's Department saying there were two people dead in the house at 17224 Dellwood Lane located in Fort Stockton, Texas. The caller said he saw a black man running from the back of the house. The caller never identified himself. Court documents and arrest reports show that fifteen minutes after the anonymous call was received, Howard Mitchel was apprehended and arrested as he was walking out of Hallstead's Pharmacy in Milltown, Texas, some forty miles away from Fort Stockton, Texas. The arresting officer was Sergeant Larry Simons, who is now Sheriff Larry Simon's of the El Paso County Sheriff's Department.

Then Sergeant Simon's arrest report shows that Howard Mitchel was arrested because he matched the description of the suspect. Which according to records, the only description received from the anonymous caller was…"The suspect was a black man." Howard Mitchel does not own a car nor does he have a driver's license. There is no way Howard could have been in Fort Stockton at 8:05 P.M. and then in Milltown at 8:20 P.M….Howard did not know why he was wrestled to the ground and handcuffed and he didn't understand why people were yelling and screaming to hang him and calling him a murderer as he was lead into the county jail.

Three hours later at 11:35 P.M., Howard Mitchel was standing in a court room in front of Judge Alberto Rivera, where he listened to a lawyer named Vernon Birchmeyer read from a criminal complaint report telling the judge of the brutal double murders Howard supposedly committed.

Court documents show...that same lawyer, Vernon Birchmeyer, told Howard that if he signed or put his mark on a piece of paper that was put in front of him, he could go back to his jail cell, after which he would be able to go home. So Howard did what the attorney asked and put his X on the paper. Howard did not have an attorney to represent him as he stood in front of the judge or when he put his X on that piece of paper, nor could he afford one. Later the judge did assign a public defender to represent Howard.

The court appointed attorney to represent Howard Mitchel's name was Barry Richards, who just happens to be the brother-in-law of then Sergeant Simons, now Sheriff Larry Simons, the man who arrested him.

All these facts that you've just read should give you pause...but as you read the rest of my report and notes, you will see how Howard Mitchel was truly innocent. He was only guilty of one thing...being a black man.

I don't know why Howard was so unlucky to be charged with these murders, but if I had to guess, it was because Howard was the first black man Sheriff Simons saw that morning. Howard was like most of the hard-working men in Milltown, Texas. He was black, poor, and uneducated.

New evidence that I uncovered during this investigation will show that Howard Mitchel was actually arrested to hide far bigger crimes...The double murders of John and Harriet Colver, and the arrest and trial of Howard Mitchel was just a cover up to hide the real crimes of money laundering and drug smuggling...My report will even sprinkle in some international action for you. You will read about Russian agents who committed multiple murders and how they started a large drug operation right here in Texas over twenty years ago. You will see how they coerced local law enforcement with huge kickbacks. Not all people in this report are bad. You will read about the many good, honest, and hard-working people in law enforcement who worked hard to dig up the truth, and we're all trying to correct a terrible wrong. I promise I will be honest with all my statements. We have brought all those involved in this wrong doing to justice.

Chapter Two
Wednesday, July 22nd, 1993

I thought I was still on vacation, but a phone call at 5:00 A.M. this morning from my boss, Deputy Director John Galone of the U.S. Marshals office in El Paso, Texas, changed all of that. I will say that he is well-respected and loved by everyone in the local law enforcement profession, including myself, but I didn't feel the love for him at the moment. I was in a deep sleep having a wild dream of being on the sidelines at a Dallas Cowboys football game, and I was with the cheerleaders doing some jumps and hugs, I don't remember dreaming of the game or even who they were playing, just the cheerleaders. The ringing of the telephone sure ended that dream.

I first met John Galone when he was my instructor when I was in the academy. Back then he was known as Professor, but his appointment by then President of the United States Gerald Ford to Deputy Director made him mine and the other 3,000 or so deputy marshals our boss and mentor. After I answered the phone, I was greeted by John telling me I was requested by higher ups to be at a meeting this morning.

"Meet me at 8:00 A.M. at the office. Clean-up, don't be late, and be on your best behavior," he said. "Rumors are that the Department of Justice has a hot case, so this could be important." Then he hung up. Not allowing me to say anything.

Now I work undercover assignments most of the time, so I usually wear blue jeans and t-shirts, so for him to say clean-up is telling me I was expected to take a shower, shave, and wear a suit and tie, which would mean the government issue dark blue suit the department gave me nine years ago. I've worn this suit to three funerals and my divorce. The rest of the time it collects dust in my closet. It's the only suit I have. To show him I was not totally disrespectful of him, I did take my shower, I did shave, but I left the makings of a goatee, and I didn't feel like wearing a suit and tie. The weather forecast today for El Paso was to be sunny and hot. One-hundred-fifteen degrees, so I put on a pair of tan slacks with a blue polo shirt. Let's face it, in my mind, I'm still on vacation. Doing my once over in front of the mirror made me feel good about myself. I thought I cleaned up pretty good considering I just had three hours of sleep. Spending the last three days at Camp Beauregard, LA for my yearly SOG schooling and tactics training. I was under the impression I still had two more days off before I was to report back to work, but the tone of the Director's voice told me not to question and just be there.

Normally the drive from my house to the El Paso County Courthouse in downtown El Paso, also known as the Lyndon B. Johnson Federal Office Building, takes me thirty-five minutes but today, thanks to a garbage truck driver who decided he wanted to be in a hurry and ended up tipping his truck over and spewing his garbage over the four lanes of traffic on Interstate 85, shutting down the south bound lanes of traffic. As I sat there listening to other cars honk their horns and drivers yelling, like that will spur the poor guys out there in this heat from the garbage company to shovel a little faster, I decided to think of what my therapist would say to me at this time, something like, "Carter, close your eyes, take some deep breathes, and try working on your patience."

I decided to turn on my radio, Country FM 103 blurted out at me, and I was listening to "On the Road Again" by Willie Nelson. The DJ was playing the song for all the cars stuck on Interstate 85. I'm glad he had a sense of humor. While I was singing, one lane finally opened, and traffic inched along, and I could turn off at the Arizona Avenue exit, which would take me right to the courthouse. I raced into the parking lot and found that it was full. I did find one space opened by the front door with a sign that said, "For Authorized Personnel Only." Well today that was me.

I checked in at the security desk in the lobby and was told I was expected in Conference Room A on the sixth floor. Normally when I report here to work, I go to the second floor. A security guard instructed me to remove all of the items in my pockets, including my gun, and place everything in a plastic container, which I was then told to set that on a conveyor belt which took the container through an x-ray-like machine with a security guard looking at a TV screen, then I was told to walk through the metal gate, then another guard waved a wand over me from head to toe. No alarms went off. Even though the same guards have seen me every day for the past eighteen years, they still do their due diligence.

After going through all the security, I was told again that I was to go directly to Conference Room A on the sixth floor. I saw the security guard pick up a clip board and put a check mark on a page and then he picked up the telephone; he saw that I was watching him and he hastily waved me through and pointed to the elevators.

Taking the elevator up, I was trying to remember what the conference room looked like. When you walk into the room, the wall on your left was full of law books from floor to ceiling. The books were overflow from the U.S. Attorney's office on the third floor.

The wall to your right has large pictures of Sam Houston and pictures of our current President and Governor, flanked by the flags of the State of Texas, a Confederate Flag, and the American Flag. Honoring the past runs deep in Texas. The wall facing you when you walk in has large windows overlooking the Rio Grande. In the center of the room is a large mahogany table with ten high back chairs.

As I walked into the conference room, I was surprised to see seven people already sitting at the table. Scanning the table, I counted six men and one woman. I started to wonder just what I did wrong to get invited to this meeting.

Deputy Director Galone walked up to me, and in his low, raspy voice, told me to keep my mouth shut and listen to everyone in the room and he would talk to me later. Usually he is the one giving all the information on new cases. I got the feeling from his stare that he wasn't impressed how I was dressed. Giving the room my once over, what surprised me was how quiet the room was.

I did notice that all the men were wearing dark blue suits, as in government issued dark blue suits. I wondered if Deputy Director Galone had called them at their home and instructed them how to dress for the occasion. I was never introduced to any of them nor did they acknowledge me, they all just sat looking straight ahead. I also noticed there were no donuts or coffee pots at the table. That might have been the reason they all looked angry. I could see the room was set up for someone to be at the head of the table, with a small table off to the side that had large stacks of legal folders and storage boxes on it.

Next I noticed Kathleen McDonald, from our U.S. Attorney's office on the third floor. She being the only female here, was sitting towards the end of the table. I started thinking maybe this meeting wasn't going to be so bad after all. I noticed Deputy Director Galone motioning for me to sit next to him, but I pretended not to notice and walked directly over and sat next to Kathleen McDonald. Now...I see her just about every morning at the elevators with the hopes of having a conversation with her. I would always say hi or good morning, and she would just look up from whatever she was reading and just smile, never saying anything to me. As I walked towards the table where she was sitting, I caught a whiff of her perfume. I noticed she was dressed in a dark-blue pant suit. Was this a female version of the government issue suit, I thought?

Pulling the chair out, I said, "Good morning." Again I noticed that perfume, and like always, she didn't say anything to me, she just smiled.

Chapter Three

Everyone just sat and stared at the empty table, nobody spoke. It was very quiet in the room. You could hear the clock on the wall ticking away the seconds. To me it was obvious we were waiting for the guest speaker, who was going to be a surprise to me because I didn't get a heads up on this meeting. It didn't take long, and we all heard the ring from the elevator and could hear the clatter of heels coming down the hallway. It sounded like two sets of shoes, and sure enough the conference room door opened, and after introductions, we were all looking at former federal prosecutor Clayton Armstrong and U.S. Assistant Attorney General Joseph Friedman. Two heavy weights from the Department of Justice and the legal profession. I also noticed they didn't have any donuts with them.

After taking time to get set up, Clayton Armstrong gave a long, chilling stare to everyone, then started by saying, "You are to take no notes of this meeting. What is said here stays here. What I am about to tell you needs to be kept in strict confidence and cannot be shared with anyone, not even staff or your family." Going over to the small table, Armstrong picked up a stack of folders and gave one to each person at the table and instructed them to open and review. On the outside of the folder was stamped "Evidence Folder" and the names John and Harriet Colver.

Inside the folder was a typed plain piece of paper with no letterhead on it that read:

Victims: John and Harriet Colver
D.O.D: April 18th, 1973
Fort Stockton, Texas

Trial: June 10th, 1973
U.S. District Judge: Alberto Rivera

Howard Mitchel, Executed, Electric Chair, May 12th, 1979.
Texas Department of Corrections, El Paso, Texas

Next in the folder were pages of black and white photos with a typed description of each on the bottom of the picture. Wedding pictures of John and Harriet Colver. Pictures of John and Harriet Colver with their two children. Joseph: D.O.B. 11/12/70 and Kathy: D.O.B. 10/7/71. Employment history of John Colver from the Fort Stockton, Texas feed mill. A copy of a property tax statement and property deed to a house that John and Harriet purchased in 1968, located in Fort Stockton, Texas. Next I was looking at a stack of black and white crime scene photos that I assumed were of John and Harriet Colver. John was tied to a kitchen chair, I could see he was tortured by being shot in both knees, with knife cuts and burn marks on his face. I could also see that his fingers were all broken. This man was tortured for hours.

From my eighteen years of working with the El Paso's Sheriff Department and the U.S. Marshals office investigating gangs and drug cases, I've seen what these drug lords and cartels can do to people when they think drugs or money have been stolen from them. I could tell someone was trying to get something from the Colver's. A bullet hole in the back of John's head was his reward for being so tough. Pictures of Harriet were just as bad. From the looks of it, the way she was on the floor, shot, beaten and stabbed, they made sure John had to watch before they killed him. There were blood splatters on the ceiling, on the kitchen cabinets, and the floor was like a lake of blood.

Over the years I've seen a lot of crime scene photos, but these were some of the worst I've ever seen. This was pre-planned torture, done by a professional killer. There were copies of newspaper articles about the case and about the arrest of Howard Mitchel in the folder also. The headlines on the first newspaper article read, "Black man seeing running from the house covered in blood, arrested by Sergeant Larry Simons of the El Paso Sheriff's Department." The article had a picture of the County Chief Medical Examiner, Doctor Leslie Adams, standing next to Simons, and they were both wearing big grins.

Under the picture was a quote by Sergeant Simons saying, "Because of the great work of the Sheriff's Department, the person that committed these terrible murders has been arrested. The community is safe again." It made me think, someone was planning to run for sheriff.

There were medical examiner reports on the Colver's, along with evidence photos showing Howard Mitchel's finger prints on the chair that John Colver was tied to, another photo showed finger prints on both the kitchen counter and the knife that was found next to Harriet Colver's body.

Next I was looking at a black and white photo of Howard Mitchel covered in blood. The photo was taken by a writer from the El Paso Free Press, showing Howard Mitchel being led from the squad car with handcuffs on into the county jail. The blood on Howard I was thinking was not from the Colver's but his own blood from the beatings I'm sure he was given. The next photo was a large black and white mug shot, taken as Howard was being booked into the county jail.

A small attempt was made to clean off the blood from his face. The photo showed a young man with short hair. You could just see the fear in his eyes. I closed my folder and leaned back in my chair. Something inside me was telling me something was not right here with these photos and this case. Armstrong made sure everyone had time to review the evidence folder. I watched as everyone completed looking at their folder. No one said anything. Was that because I was not the only one who was thinking something was not right here, I asked myself.

Armstrong again made sure everyone had looked at the first folder. He did not say anything or take questions, he just walked over to the small table and grabbed another stack of folders and passed these to each of us. Inside this folder was just a one-page document with Department of Justice letterhead.

"DEPARTMENT OF JUSTICE"
TOP SECRET ONLY

EXTRADITION PAPERS

United States of America
VS
Petre Navitscof
Nedia Petrov
John Doe

Again Armstrong waited until everyone had looked at this folder, then he said, "We will discuss this form at our next meeting." Saying his intention is to file this at a later date. Armstrong continued by saying, "I will now tell you what the Department of Justice knows about the life and the murders of John and Harriet Colver."

I will say this about Clayton Armstrong, he knew how to take control of a room. All this time Armstrong had been standing by the head of the table, where he had all his notes and storage boxes stacked up, but now he started to walk towards the back of the room, making everyone twist and turn in their chairs to watch him. He had everyone's attention, that was for sure.

When he got to the back of the room, he reached into his shirt pocket and pulled out a pack of cigarettes and put one to his lips, he fumbled with a match book, and as he struck the match, I could smell the sulfur from the match and see the glow of his face. He was taking his time as he lit his cigarette. Everyone's eyes were glued to him.

As he exhaled the smoke, he said, "We know that John and Harriet Colver's actual names were Max and Olga Mikhailov. Both were chemists and nuclear scientists. Both were born in Russia and were trained as Russian agents. They were planted in Fort Stockton, Texas in 1968 by the Russian government to gather information on the nuclear power plants in Bay City, Texas and Glen Rose, Texas."

Armstrong blew out another cloud of smoke and now started walking to the front of the room, causing all of us to turn and twist again in our chairs to follow him. He stopped in front of the bank of windows that looked out at the Rio Grande.

He stood looking for a second or two, he blew out another puff of smoke from his cigarette, and as he turned to face us, he continued by saying, "In 1970 we turned the Colver's into double agents, and for over three years they were our top agents, sending false information back to Russia on the two nuclear power plants. I was their handler and many times they put their lives in danger. John and Harriet always wanted to stay in the United States. To be free. They loved Fort Stockton. They also loved their mother country, Russia, but did not like the political infighting that was making their country so poor."

"A footnote to that time," Armstrong said as he exhaled his last puff of smoke before he crushed out the cigarette in the ash tray,

"In the late 1960's through the 1980's, we were in the middle of a Geo Political race with Russia and China in the development of nuclear power plants. Russia in particular was giving both states of Texas and Florida large interest on the development of their nuclear power plants and their reactors. Causing both states to go on high alert many times. The information we were sending to Russia through the Colver's seemed to be helping defuse most of the tension," Armstrong said in a softer than usual voice. I sensed a sadness about him as he was talking about the Colver's. He must have gotten very close to them.

Armstrong also noted, "After the April 26th, 1986 Chernobyl nuclear power plant explosion in Ukraine, where their number four reactor cracked and dumped huge amounts of radiation into the atmosphere, Russia, China, and the United States all started the Nuclear Safety Council and established safety standards and a treaty where we share information that is still being practiced today. The FBI and Justice Department closed all active files on the Colver's in 1974," Armstrong continued. "We thought there was no need to have an open case following their murders."

Armstrong looked up to all of us and said, "That all changed three weeks ago." Armstrong seemed to take his time looking over his notes. "A Mrs. Maria DelMoto contacted our FBI office here in El Paso. She and her husband purchased the house at 17234 Dellwood Lane in Fort Stockton, Texas, which just happens to be across the street from where the Colver's lived. The Colver's address was 17224 Dellwood Lane. While remodeling the house," he read on, "Mr. DelMoto found a cardboard box in the attic of the garage that was mailed by Mrs. Colver to the previous home owners, a Mr. and Mrs. John Silva. From what we can deduct, the Colver's and the Silva's were close friends. According to Mrs. DelMoto, the box was never opened and somehow was left in the attic by the previous home owners." Armstrong stopped at this point, asked if there were any questions, which there were none. I wasn't surprised as I'm thinking everyone was sitting at the edge of their seats waiting for the rest of the story. Armstrong did take the time to light up another cigarette. I don't smoke, but I felt I could have used one right now also.

Armstrong continued by saying, "Mrs. DelMoto told our agents she was thinking she had found a hidden treasure when she found the box, but after she opened the box, she was surprised at what she was looking at. Inside was a diary that belonged to Harriet Colver." Armstrong walked over to the small table and reached into one of the storage boxes and held up a small pink diary.

"When Mrs. DelMoto called our local FBI office, she was very adamant that someone look at this diary because it has information on death threats the Colver's were receiving. Our agents did contact Mrs. DelMoto and were given this diary, which shows Harriet made daily entries from December 18th, 1972 to April 15th, 1973. The last entry was made just three days before their murder. Harriet writes they are receiving phone calls and people were coming to their house late at night threatening them. She writes how she and John fear for their lives. Not because of their nuclear power plant assignment or threats from Russian, but because of the threats from strangers, who were demanding they turn over a package of cash...Harriet writes that she and John keep saying there must be a mistake. They know nothing about a package of cash. Harriet writes she did not know who they can trust because the person who keeps coming to their house and threatening them is a police officer. A woman police officer." Armstrong removed his glasses and looked at everyone at the table.

"I'm directing FBI Special Agent in Charge Edward LaPinta," as he pointed to one of the blue suits at the end of the table, "to read this diary written by Harriet Colver and to find out about this package of cash and look into who this mysterious woman police officer is."

Armstrong then went to the small table, picked up one storage box, and set it in front of LaPinta and told him all the information he would need to investigate is in this box.

Armstrong continued, "Next I want to review the arrest and trial of Howard Mitchel. I am also aware that six of the jurors have died of unnatural causes. The evidence files show all six were tortured and killed, like the Colver's were. All six cases are still open with no leads. Added to that mess, the lead prosecutor, a Vernon Birchmeyer, died when his car exploded in his garage. We have no strong leads in any of these cases. I'm directing the U.S. Marshals office, in particular Deputy Marshal Ryan Carter, to be agent in charge of this investigation. I want the six unsolved cases of the jurors and the death of Vernon Birchmeyer's investigated. I want protection to the remaining jurors, along with protection to Judge Alberto Rivera." Armstrong then pointed to the small table, looked at me, and said, "Those three boxes are information you will need about the jurors, the Judge, and the trial."

Before I could make an acknowledgement, Armstrong started sorting through his notes again and said, "I'm also placing Ms. McDonald from our U.S. Attorney's office under the umbrella of the U.S. Marshals office." Armstrong kept reading from his notes saying he wanted her to work with the agents when they interview all personnel about the six unsolved jurors and the Birchmeyer's case. "I also want her to set up a meeting with the group known as the Legal Justice For

All group. I want both agents, LaPinta and Carter, there also with Ms. McDonald when she meets with that group." Armstrong looked up from his notes and said, "They say they have information on this case. I want to know what that information is." Armstrong then asked if there were any questions. And like robots, we all shook our heads no.

Armstrong then gave agent LaPinta, Chief Deputy Galone, myself, and Ms. McDonald his business card.

"Call me at any time if you have any problems. This is top priority. All other cases are on the back burner." I noticed his office was at 1700 Pennsylvania Avenue. Washington D.C., the White House.

Armstrong then went back to the head of the table and started filing his papers back into his briefcase and said in a very stern voice, "I want timely updates from this team. This is an important case to me, so I will expect results. We will meet in this room one week from today at 8:00 sharp." It was kind of strange, but to me it looked like he was looking straight at me when he said that. Like he knew my reputation of always being late.

Clayton Armstrong and Simon Friedman both walked out of the room. My head was still spinning. I didn't hear the clatter from their shoes in the hallway, but I did hear the elevator bell as the door opened and closed to take them down to the main floor.

Chapter Four
Wednesday, October 14th, 1993

I stayed seated while everyone else left the room. I was thinking about everything Armstrong just presented. I had more questions than answers. One of them was the "Top Secret Only" form from the Department of Justice with the two Russian names on it for extradition. Armstrong never discussed that. Was that on purpose? I was getting that itchy feeling like we weren't getting all the information. Which was typical with the feds. Working with the FBI has always been stressful. I was hoping working with agent LaPinta would be different. But now add working with a Department of Justice team, that makes it a whole new ball game, I thought. I really wasn't too excited about working with either agency.

I was kind of excited to be working with the ADA office though. Especially Kathleen McDonald. My train of thought was broken when the chair next to me moved and I was looking at my boss Deputy Director Galone.

"Welcome to the big leagues, your ass is in the hot seat now," he said with a smile. "You better ask your therapist for more stress pills," he continued laughing. "You're going to need them." It's rare that I see Deputy Director Galone laugh. That was telling me how bad this was going to be.

"Let's meet tomorrow morning and go over everything that will be needed," he said as he got up from his chair.

I shook my head in agreement and told him, "I was going to tear into some of the boxes now and look at the files on the jurors. Just to get a head start on everything." We both agreed we should keep using this conference room as our meeting place. As he was walking out of the room, he said he would reach out to the FBI Director and coordinate meetings with them and get back to me.

I walked over to the small table that the boxes were on, opening them. I found the one that had the files from the jury pool. Going back to the conference table, I spread all the files out in front of me. Each juror had an individual file with their juror number that was assigned to them by the jury pool, along with miscellaneous background information.

A recap form from the pool read as follows:

Jury Pool No:	Juror Name:
P 002	Susan Gallagher
P 004	Helen Grims
P 005	Victor McDermott
P 007	Edward Bell
HP 008	Kenneth Wilson
HP 009	Joseph Tate
P 011	Johnny Morris
HP 013	Doris Harper
P 014	Clyde Williams
HP 015	Howard Baker
HP 017	James Devale
HP 018	Donald Lampley

No alternate jurors needed was typed on the bottom of the list.

Flipping through the stacks of paper, I noticed eighteen jurors from the pool were interviewed by both the court appointed Public Defender Barry Richards and the Lead Prosecutor Vernon Birchmeyer, and from that process, the final twelve jurors were selected. A question I was going to ask Ms. McDonald was what does the letters P and HP stand for on the recap assignment form?

In all my years that I've been in law enforcement, my experience in jury selection is limited, but every case that I have been involved with, the court usually sets aside at least two weeks to select a jury. Sometimes interviewing up to 100 jurors from the pool is not uncommon. Especially a high-profile murder case as this was. This case took just one day for the jury selection while interviewing only eighteen jurors from the pool. That was a big red flag for me. Another one to add to my "to be asked questions".

My next big red flag was when I saw Barry Richards was the court appointed public defender assigned by the Judge to defend Howard Mitchel. Barry Richards I know is the brother-in-law to the Sheriff in the case. Larry Simons was the one who made the arrest of Howard Mitchel. I put that on my list also.

Next I pulled out the list of the six deceased jurors that Clayton Armstrong gave me and compared it to the list from the jury pool.

Kenneth Wilson	DOD 3/11/1980	Newman City, Tx	El Paso Tx County
Joseph Tate	DOD 9/12/1982	Horizon City, Tx	El Paso Tx County
Doris Harper	DOD 6/04/1981	Clint, Tx	El Paso Tx County
Howard Baker	DOD 2/22/1984	Canutillo, Tx	El Paso Tx County
James Devale	DOD 7/16/1988	San Elizario, Tx	El Paso Tx County
Donald Lampley	DOD 11/03/1985	El Paso, Tx	El Paso Tx County

I went back to the small table and found the storage box that had the evidence files from the local police departments and the Sheriff's Department that would have investigated the six murders of the jurors. I also found the folder on the death of the Lead Prosecutor of the case, Vernon Birchmeyer, who died on May 12th, 1993.

As I matched the jury pool folders to the evidence folders, I made several notes:

1) All cases were in El Paso County, which meant that Sheriff Larry Simons investigated or was in charge of each investigation.

2) The Sheriff's Department moved all six murders of the jurors, along with lead prosecutor Vernon Birchmeyer, case to the inactive but still open and unsolved cases on May 13th, 1993, just one day after Vernon Birchmeyer was killed.

3) I noticed Doctor Leslie Adams, the Chief Medical Examiner for the county, signed all deaths certificates and performed the autopsies that were needed. Which is not unusual. I expected to see his signature on all the death certificates. I just made a note of it.

4) Matching the pool assignment form to the list of suspicious deaths list from Armstrong, I noticed all six of the unsolved jurors deaths have letters HP in front of their name, while everyone else has a P in front in front of their name.

Next I picked up the telephone that was on the table and dialed extension 003, which connected me to the Sheriff's Department on the ground floor. I told myself that to get this ball rolling, I will have to start with the Sheriff's Department. After the phone rang three times, Sheriff's assistant Betty Lou Quantel answered.

I first met Betty Lou when I was hired into the Sheriff's Department eighteen years ago, when I was a young, cocky, know it all rookie. She was a patrol sergeant then. Everyone in the department loved and feared her. I know she saved or covered my ass many times. Even after I transferred to the Marshals office, we still kept in touch. She was at my wedding, and seven years later she consoled me at my divorce. She was even at the hospital for three straight days while I recovered from being shot nine years ago, and I'm her oldest son Robert's Godfather. So you see what I mean, she is like family to me.

Betty Lou makes my job easier. If I ever have any questions or problems on a case or need a special favor, I felt I could call her, and because she's been in the department for almost thirty years, she knew everyone and everything.

I started the conversation with, "Hi, Betty, long time no see, how ya been?" After a couple of minutes of her telling me all her problems at home with her husband, kids, grandkids, and her dog, she said she would like to meet in the cafeteria sometime for lunch. She said she's been meaning to call me because she has something important to tell me. I told her I could come down right now if she wanted, but she informed me that it was almost 6:00 and we should all go home now, it could wait till another day.

I told her, "I've just been assigned this huge case, but as soon as I wrap it up, we can get together."

She told me she heard that I had special visitors this morning. "They were from Washington the scuttle butt is saying." Nothing happens in this courthouse without Betty Lou hearing about it. "Everyone in the courthouse was talking about it this afternoon. Sounds like you're moving up in the world, Carter," she said with a laugh. Changing the conversation back to business, I told her I've been assigned to investigate some open and unsolved cases. I gave her the names of the cases and told her I would need all the county files on them. Betty Lou asked if this was what the big shots from Washington was here for. I ignored the question, and I could hear her writing down the names as I gave them to her, she repeated each name, making sure of the correct spelling.

"So tell me, are these old cases what Washington was here for?" she asked again with a little excitement in her voice.

I told her I've been sworn to secrecy and I really can't talk about the case right now. She quickly dropped the conversation and said she would take care of all the paperwork that is required by the county when any case file leaves the Sheriff's office, and she would have everything ready to be picked up in the morning.

We ended the conversation with me saying, "Thank you, you're the best, and I'll get back to you on the lunch." And she said, "Be safe, Ryan," and hung up.

I leaned back in my chair and closed my eyes. It felt good to relax. I started to think of everything that happened today. Clayton Armstrong blew in and made it a whirlwind of a day. I looked up at the clock above the door, and it said it was 6:30 P.M.

"How did this day go so fast?" I said out loud. I was tired, but I still wanted to look at some more files before I called it a day, so I got up and walked over to the small table and grabbed a stack of folders from the last storage box.

All the files from the three storage boxes were now on the table. This last box was all on the Howard Mitchel case. I walked back to the table and started reading the reports and looking at all the photos. I must have really got engrossed in the files because the next thing I knew, the conference room doors opened and in walked five cleaning ladies with their carts of brooms, mops, and vacuum cleaners. The clock on the wall above the door said it was 11:45 P.M. This was the evening cleaning crew. They were as surprised to see me here this late as I was to see them. They were all talking at once trying to tell me they were taking their lunch break and they always eat in this room.

I stood up and introduced myself and slid the files to the end of the table and told them to go ahead and sit and eat. Their thirty-minute lunch break was full of their laughs and them talking in Spanish and then looking at me, then laughing some more.

I enjoyed their company, but I had to tell them that after tonight, this room will be restricted and will always be locked. They would not be allowed back in here. I think they understood, but I made a note for Deputy Director Galone to pass that info on to the powers that be. After the cleaning ladies left, I rearranged all the files back on the table. Looking up at the clock, it now said 12:30 A.M. There was no way I could focus anymore on the files, I was just too tired. So I turned off the lights and locked the door and went home. Aware that this will be another night of short sleep.

Chapter Five
Thursday, July 23rd, 1993

The next morning while driving to the courthouse, I started thinking of what my day had in store for me. First, I was to meet with my boss and go over the security detail of the still living jurors and Judge at 8:00. Second, I would be meeting with FBI agent Edward LaPinta sometime in the morning. The two of us would go over all the files I looked at last night and come up with some kind of game plan. I also had high hopes I would be seeing ADA Kathleen McDonald. As tired as I was, I was really looking forward to talking to her and her talking to me for once. What I was not expecting was having Sheriff Larry Simons waiting for me at the security desk in the lobby.

After making some small talk with security officer, Henry Bates, he always says, "Good morning, Ryan, it's going to be a beautiful day." He has been saying that to me for the past twelve years. He then asks me to place all my items from my pockets, along with my revolver, into a plastic container, which he then sends through a scanner. I then walk through the metal detector, hopefully without it making any noise. Then Henry always asks me to show him my ID, which whenever I'm in the building I am to have clipped to my shirt or jacket to verify that I am Ryan Carter, U.S. Marshals office. He has been trained to do that to everyone before they can enter the building.

As I was removing my items from the plastic container, shaking my head thinking of the ordeal I just went through, Sheriff Simons walked up to me and asked if we could go into the small conference room at the end of the hall for a little chat. Following him down the hall, I knew I was in store for one of his famous "Rath of God" yelling tantrums. I was not disappointed.

I just barely walked into the conference room, and he got right into my face demanding to know why I was investigating some of his old cases. My silence, along with my natural smirk on my face, seemed to add fuel to his fire.

"Well, Sheriff, I can't get into specifics, but I can tell you my orders came right from the Department of Justice and the White House." He gave me a look of I don't believe you. I pointed for him to take a chair and sit. "I can't go into details with you today, Larry." I thought I would use his first name so as to calm him down a little. "But I will be honest with you, there are some of your old cases I've been requested to look into."

"Do I need to get an attorney?" he asked. For the first time since I've known Sheriff Larry Simons, he looked scared. He lost his "Rath of God" attitude that he had when we walked into the room and now he just looked small and defeated.

"At this point, we're just looking and reviewing cases. In a day or so, I will be calling you in to be interviewed. As you know, you will have the right to have an attorney with you for that."

He just sat there not moving, it looked as if he just aged ten years right in front of me. His face turning from deep red to a pale white. He was looking right at me, like he was in a trance, his eyes never blinking. He started rocking back and forth in the chair. The chair making creaking sounds like it was going to break. I also couldn't stop watching him wringing his hands like they were in water. I was becoming concerned that he might be having a heart attack. I started feeling sorry for him. His wife had just died a couple of months ago from cancer. Out of respect, I went to that funeral. I remember seeing him crying at the cemetery. So out of character for him. He stood up and walked to the door.

Stopping he turned and said, "Thank you for being honest with me, Ryan. Let me know when you want that interview, and I'll be there. And those files you requested are ready for you to pick up." And he opened the door and walked out. I just stood there thinking, in all the years that I've worked with him, he has never called me by my first name. It was always Carter or something with a little profanity. After he left the room, I felt sick to my stomach. I didn't really like the man, but seeing the blood drain from his face like that was horrifying to me. Moments like this made me not to like my job.

I quickly left the room and ran down the hall to the elevator and went straight to the sixth floor. Walking into the conference room, I was met by a very impatient Deputy Director Galone, my boss. I looked at the clock on the wall, that I had just spent the last sixteen plus hours looking at, and I could see it was 8:20 A.M., which meant I was twenty minutes late for our meeting, and I knew I was in trouble. One of Deputy Director John Galone's many famous trademarks was to always be punctual, which he also expected everyone else to be. I knew I was going to get lectured again by him, and I knew just what he was going to say. That I needed to be more responsible and respectful to others but especially to him. And when I have an 8:00 appointment with him, I God damn better be on time.

"I swear, Carter, you're going to be late to your own God damn funeral." Yes, I knew exactly what he was going to say. We've had this talk many times over the years. But I cut him off before he could start. I started talking very fast and I told him how I just left Sheriff Simons in the lobby.

I told him the whole conversation, along with Sheriff Simon's reactions. I knew there was no love between the Sheriff and the Director, but I could see the concern on his face. Any more conversation we would have had about the sheriff stopped because just at that moment, in walked FBI agent LaPinta, along with ADA McDonald, for our 8:00 meeting.

I was waiting for him to lecture them, but he didn't, he just turned to me and said, "Let's pick this conversation up later," he said and gave me his famous stare.

We all walked to the conference table and sat down. It took a couple of minutes for everyone to get comfortable, but we quickly got to business. Because my therapist says I have this "Need to be in charge personality," I quickly started the meeting with how we will start by reviewing the murder, arrest, and trial of Howard Mitchel per the request of Clayton Armstrong. I told them how I emptied all three of the storage boxes and stacked the files in order on the table.

I pointed to the stack of the individual jury pool files at the end of the table and said, "I've read all of these files and I've made notes of concerns or questions that I have and that I would like to go over." I started off with how I was concerned, how a jury selection for a trial of this magnitude could take just one day.

I handed the Jury pool recap assignment list to both LaPinta and ADA McDonald, and as they were looking at the list, they both agreed with me that one day was very fast and unusual.

While they were studying the list of names on the assignment form, I pointed out to them the pool numbering system, which had either a P or HP in front of each name.

ADA McDonald said, "I know what this means, and it is very unusual. It's something that the Texas courts allowed years ago, but it's not allowed in today's cases." While she still was looking at the assignment list and looking concerned, McDonald continued on with, "The P meant the juror was selected from the pool of available jurors while the HP means the juror was handpicked or recommended by someone."

We all looked at her like she was making that up.

"What do you mean, handpicked?" I replied.

"I never knew that was ever possible. It's hard to believe," the Director said.

McDonald continued with, "Anyone, a Senator, a Judge, hell, for that matter a Mr. or Mrs. common civilian years ago could made a request to the Governor who they would like to see in a jury box for a certain trial, through writing of course." We all know how with just a flick of a pen, a governor can even today have someone released from prison and have their record expunged."

She stopped talking and did that pause for effect thing, like she was lecturing us. She continued with, "Well, with that same flick of a pen, the governor, years ago, could have someone assigned to a jury. It didn't happen all that often," she said, "and it was rare when it did happen, but it did. Usually if the person who's making the request is in the same political party or a big donor to the governor, the request pretty much got rubber stamped. Especially if it was in a reelection year." We all just sat there, looking at her, having a hard time believing what she just said. In all my years working in the courthouse, I never heard about this. McDonald said she thinks the state senate took that privilege away from the Governor's office maybe ten years ago. There are a lot of old Texas state laws that most people don't know about and would be surprised if they knew about them.

To prove her point, she reached over the table and picked up the phone and dialed the clerk of courts' office, saying she knows they still have all their files and documents from the last twenty years ago available for us to see and said she will request copies of the signed court forms that would have been required back then. After a couple of moments, she said she was on hold and it was going to take a while for them to find the signed forms and for me to continue.

I continued on with, "The six jurors who were murdered all had an HP in front of their names." I turned back to my notes and said, "Another thing I noticed was that the court appointed public defender for Howard Mitchel was Barry Richards, who I know is Sheriff Larry Simon's brother-in-law."

Everyone's eye brows went up with that information. "That connection to the Sheriff, or the arresting sergeant as he was known back then, was never mentioned in the case and is very unusual and would be considered very unethical," McDonald said, still holding the phone to her ear and said she knows that her office is investigating Barry Richards for fraud and said his law license has been suspended many times by the State of Texas over the years. Her office has always been wondering who was always covering for him. Charges always seemed to get dropped against him.

LaPinta was wondering if the Judge at the time knew about this. McDonald quickly shot her hand up for silence, and she was writing down information she was receiving from the person on the phone. We were all staring at her, anxious to hear what she was being told.

We could hear her saying, "Okay...okay...well that was fast... really," then she said, "Yes, I would like all these copies sent to my office. Yes, today would be great. Thank you," and hung up.

McDonald slid back into her chair, and with a big smile, said, "Well that phone call was interesting." She leaned forward in her chair and said, "Talking to Wendy in the Clerk of Courts office, she found the signed request form for the six handpicked jurors for the Howard Mitchel's trial, and guess whose signature is on the request?" We were all looking at her with total excitement in our faces, like kids at Christmas, but she was looking at us like she expected us to pay her for the information...I bet she was evil as a kid, I thought...but all we had to do was wait her out because she couldn't hold back the exciting news. "Wendy said she was expecting to see our Governor's signature on the form but," McDonald said slowly...stretching this conversation out...but looking disappointed we didn't play her game, finally said, "Instead a Betty Lou Quantel from our Sheriff's department signed her name for the Governor approving the selection of the six hand-picked jurors. Wendy does not know how nobody noticed that the Governor did not sign the form. It definitely was not a legally signed request." McDonald continued with, "And I was not the first person to ask to look at this jury assignment request."

Again there was this pause for effect moment.

McDonald was again playing her game and looking at us like she just let out a fart in church, her face was red, and she had this little devilish grin, but she just couldn't hold back her excitement any longer, and she blurred out, "Our Sheriff, Larry Simons," she said, almost yelling it out. "He asked Wendy this morning if he could have the case file on the Howard Mitchel's case. But according to Wendy, Sheriff Simons never showed up to look at the file. That's why we got this information so fast," she said excitedly. "The file was still on Wendy's desk."

"Now why would Betty Lou Quantel put her signature on a jury assignment form, and better yet, why would Sheriff Simons request to look at this jury assignment file today?" I shouted.

I next turned to LaPinta and asked him if he had any information on the items Armstrong requested the FBI to investigate, which included the four-million dollars the Colver's were demanded to turn over, find the identity of this mysterious police office, and read and analyze the diary.

His response surprised me. He stood up, and looking like he was thinking or in deep thought about something, finally said, "I have information on all three items...plus I think an additional one...We have figured out where the four-million dollars came from, but we don't know where it is right now and how it connects to this case."

He looked around at everyone at the table looking for a question from us, and when nobody said anything, he continued with, "Okay then...do you know what happens to all the evidence on a drug case after the case is closed?"

This time I did respond by saying, "When I worked in the sheriff's office, I knew all seized cars, boats, and houses were turned over to the county after the case was closed to be sold at auction. While all cash recovered in drug raids goes directly into the county budget and all drugs recovered goes to Laughlin Air Force Base to the incinerator to be destroyed." LaPinta, looking at me and shaking his head in agreement, continued, "FBI agents assigned to this case stumbled on old cash receipt vouchers from the County Admin Department. They're like the bookkeepers for the county," he said.

"Their records show that from 1969 through 1980, the period in question here, the county records show a little over nine-million dollars of cash from drug raids was recorded into the county budget, but when we go over the case files in the Sheriff's Department for that same period, their records show that over thirteen-million dollars cash was seized. This thirteen-million dollars is the amount of money that should have been turned over to the County and entered into the county budget."

"Leaving four million dollars difference," we both said. "So where did that money go?"

Deputy Director Galone said, "We're still looking into that."

LaPinta said, "But that's not all, we found more problems. As for the diary, when we picked it up, it was still in the cardboard box that showed it was mailed to John and Phyllis Silva at 17234 Dellwood Lane, which is the house next to the Colver's. A couple of interesting things here," he said. "First, when we ran a background check on John and Phyllis Silva, there is no information on them before 1968. It's like they didn't exist before then. Second, the diary does show where Harriet describes receiving late night visits and phone calls from a lady police officer. Harriet is adamant she knows nothing about a large package of cash and keeps telling that to the officer. She writes she's getting scared because the police officer is mentioning she knows Harriet's children and hopes no harm comes to them. We're still looking into who this female police officer is," he continued. "The list is short because there just wasn't a lot of female police officers back then." LaPinta continued on with his report by saying, "That brings me to the additional and most interesting items we found. While the FBI was looking into the records of seized cash that was turned over to the county, we also noticed discrepancies on the amount of cocaine and marijuana that county records show being logged in and out of the evidence room.

Again, when we take the Sheriff's arrest files and match that to the county evidence room records and compare them both to what was logged into Laughlin Air Force Base to be incinerated, we find huge differences. Large amounts of cocaine and marijuana are leaving the county evidence room but not making it to Laughlin Air Force Base," he said.

LaPinta explained, "All evidence is recorded and signed in by the arresting officer who gives full details of everything being turned into the evidence room. All drugs are measured down to the ounce and is verified by the arresting officer and the desk sergeant.

When drugs leave the evidence room and are shipped to Laughlin Air Force Base to the incinerator, the desk sergeant and either the

Sheriff or a Sheriff designate verify what is leaving the evidence room. The drugs are loaded onto trucks that are owned by Apache Transport Inc., which is the contracted company the county uses for special runs like this. The drugs are transported in a motorcade of two sheriff's squads and the Apache Transport trucks to Laughlin Air Force Base. The drug shipment is again verified by the drivers of the trucks and the guard at the base."

LaPinta was turning pages of notes over and stopped when he found the page he was looking for.

After taking a huge breath, he then exhaled and continued, "Laughlin Air Force Base is using a private security company, known as All Safe Security Company, at all low-level locations on the base. Believe it or not, the incinerator loading dock is considered one of these low-level locations," LaPinta said with a smirk on his face. This created a stir from everyone, as it was hard to believe. LaPinta held up his hand for us to calm down, so he could continue speaking. "This is where it gets interesting," LaPinta said.

"Earlier I ordered background checks on the six deceased jurors, which gave us answers to some of our questions. First I found that all six deceased jurors worked for Apache Transport at the same time. Remember that's the trucking company the county hires to transport the drugs to Laughlin Air Force Base incinerator," he said "Second, All Safe Security Company was not cooperative with me when I asked for their company records. I was met by the President of the company, a Mr. Michael Mancini and his attorney...the one and only...Barry Richards."

LaPinta looked up from his notes, which allowed everyone to say in unison, "What?"

He gave everyone a couple of moments to calm down and said, "Why does his name keep showing up in this case?" He continued by saying, "I was told by Mr. Mancini that it would not be in the best interest of his company to turn over any documents to the FBI at this time. And in a polite way, I was asked to leave. So this morning, I went back to their corporate offices at 6:00 A.M. with a subpoena in hand and picked up twenty-seven boxes of company records. I was met at the door by a Melania Garza, a cleaning lady. She was as cooperative as she could be, but being a cleaning lady, she didn't have much information about the company. She did call her boss, Mr. Mancini, who showed up within ten minutes. After a short tantrum, he calmed down and let me know his attorney would be calling me. I told Mr. Mancini that I also would be calling Mr. Richards later today.

I immediately brought all the files to my office and came straight to this meeting, only spending about twenty minutes looking at some of the records. But after listening to ADA McDonald earlier go over what was found by the Clerk of Courts department showing how Betty Lou Quantel from our Sheriff's department had signed the necessary forms to have all six, now deceased jurors assign to the Howard Mitchel case, a bell went off in my head. I remembered seeing the name Quantel in one of the payroll ledgers of prior employees," he said as he picked up a large thick folder and held it up for all to see. "According to their records, a George Quantel worked for them as a guard at Laughlin Air Force Base at the incinerator loading dock. That job makes him the one who inspects and signs in all delivery trucks from Apache Transport," he said. "What are the odds that he's related to our Betty Lou Quantel in the Sheriff's Department?" he asked. At this point, I felt I needed to tell everyone my connections to the Quantel family.

I ended up saying, "Working with Betty Lou almost daily for eighteen years, I always felt she was the most honest person I knew." I told them how, after I was shot, she stayed at the hospital with me for three days, making sure I was okay. "I love her like a sister, and I can't believe she would intentionally do anything dishonest. I was not as familiar with George, but he always seemed like a great husband and a good family man. "

LaPinta made sure I was finished talking and gave me a couple of moments to compose myself.

As he walked back to his chair and sat down, he said, "We show no personal connections of Betty Lou Quantel to All Safe Security Company or Apache Transport Inc.," he said looking at me. "But we do need to ask why she signed her name for the Governor, approving the selection of the six handpicked jurors." I had to agree.

Deputy Director Galone spoke up then and said, "I think we're ready to set up some interviews. Let's not wait. Given the importance of this investigation that Washington is laying on us, I don't think we need to be polite with these people. So tell our Sheriff and both George and Betty Lou Quantel and also Barry Richards the attorney that they are to be here, in this room, tomorrow morning at 8:00. I want this to happen tomorrow." He continued on by saying, "Instruct them that tomorrow's interviews will be on the arrest and trial of Howard Mitchel."

"Also," he continued, "let them know if they want an attorney with them, that would be a wise decision. And if they do not show up, an arrest warrant will be issued."

He was looking at ADA McDonald when he said all that, and to her credit, I watched her writing everything down and then said, "I will take care of it, Chief." That brought our first group meeting to an end, and I for one thought today was very productive. Working with LaPinta so far was okay. I was surprised he seemed to be focused on the case and was very thorough.

After everyone left the room, I started to recap in my mind everything that was said today. I remembered when LaPinta was telling me about the seized assets, like houses, cars, and boats the county inherits after cases are closed. At the time, I made a mental note to look at all properties, as in houses that were seized by the DEA and the County from 1969 to 1980.

I picked up the phone and called LaPinta at his office and I felt lucky that he was still at work and he answered. After we said our pleasantries and talked about today's sit down, I told him what I was thinking of.

"Do you remember when you were telling me about the nine-million dollars the County posted into their budget from 1969 to 1980?" I asked. "I was wondering, did you get any information about the houses that were seized in that period?" I could hear him shuffling through papers, and he replied his search request was for cash only. His thinking at the time was that this case revolved around the four-million dollars in cash the Colver's were being threatened about.

I told him, "I really don't have any strong thoughts of why I'm asking about seized houses, but something is just nagging at me, and I'm just curious." I will give LaPinta credit, he didn't hesitate and said he will put in another request and would get back to me.

Looking at the clock on the wall, I could see it was 6:15. I said to myself it's time to go home. Thursday night football tonight with my beloved Cowboys playing the Redskins. I just had time to pick up a pizza and get home to watch the game.

Chapter Six

Standing and looking through the double doors that opened to the south parking lot. I could see it had rained earlier. And it looked like it rained a lot, I thought. The glow from the parking lot lights told me the rain has now turned into a mist. Texas rain storms usually are quick, and it's not uncommon to get two to four inches of rain in a couple of hours. Almost always causing floods. Today was no exception. Looking over the parking lot, it looked like a large lake with my car parked in the middle. It has been said many times by me, and always out of anger, about the flaws in the design of our parking lot. Whenever it rains, the water flows towards the storm drain, which is a good thing and that's what it's supposed to do, but the one drain the county engineer thought was good enough doesn't and can't accept the water fast enough, causing it to back up and always making a lake out of the parking lot.

On a day like this, you can tell who the thinkers and planners of the world are. They're the ones smart enough to have umbrellas with them and have tall rubber boots on, making the walk to their car easier and not as stressful.

The ones that are not so gifted in the thinking or planning department were standing next to me, plotting out a course that would be needed to get to our cars. Seeing that I didn't have an umbrella or tall rubber boots or a boat, I didn't see any hope of saving my shoes and socks from a soaking they were about to receive.

I thought of the Bible where Jesus parted the seas, or where he actually walked on water. I waited for a moment, hoping for a sign that my request for a miracle would be granted, and when it wasn't, I shrugged my shoulders and decided it was time for me to go. I bolted out the door and started to run. I was hoping nobody was watching as I started skipping, sometimes on my tip toes through the water.

About halfway to my car, I stopped running and accepted the fact that I might as well look manly about the situation and just walk through the lake instead of looking like a ballet dancer. I was just about to climb into my car when I heard my name called out, and to my surprise, Assistant District Attorney Kathleen McDonald was running towards me carrying her umbrella and wearing a pair of bright yellow rubber boots. I wasn't surprised to see that she was one of the gifted planners and thinkers of the world. Standing in front of me and struggling to catch her breath, she said the District Attorney thought it would be a good idea if she could be with me when I interview Judge Alberto Rivera.

I assured her that after tomorrow morning's interview with the Quantels, the Sheriff, and Barry Richards, I was planning on calling the Judge and would be setting up a time to meet with him. And I told her I was happy to have her with. She just stood there looking up at me, not saying anything else. Just shaking her head up and down, like she was saying yes. I was hoping she wanted to say more. I just didn't want this moment to end.

It's funny, I thought, every morning when I would see her by the elevators, my mind always had the right words to say to her. I always felt like I wanted to sweep her into my arms and dance with her like they did in the old-time movies, ending the dance with a kiss and her telling me how much she loves me. I know it was a dream, but it felt so real. While I was shaking my head to get out of my dream and get back to the moment, I could see she was still looking at me, and she was giving me a strange look, causing me to get a little excited, then I noticed she was pointing, and to my disappointment, she was pointing to the car that was parked next to mine, telling me that was her car and she needed me to move so she could get into her car.

Awe, yes, so much for my dream of a dance and a kiss.

As I watched her dig for her car keys from her purse, I thought to myself, what is it with women having large purses? I also just noticed she had changed her clothes, and I could see she was now wearing a Washington Redskins football sweater.

I heard myself blurt out, "I like your car." Sounding like a high school kid talking to a girl for the first time. She didn't even look at me, she just started her car up. As I stood and really took a look at her car, I could see it was a rusty, banged up, army green 1974 Ford Pinto with a Bill Clinton and Al Gore presidential sticker on it. The car started with a loud roar from the muffler, and it coughed out a big black cloud of smoke. I could tell she was embarrassed, so I thought I should change the subject.

"How about those Redskins?" I yelled over the sound of the loud muffler, thinking because she was wearing a Washington Redskin sweatshirt she was a fan. "They sure have a good team this year, don't they?" I struggled to say.

Being a die-hard fan of the Cowboys, it was painful for me to say anything positive about the Washington Redskins. Washington has not won a game so far this year, their record is 0 – 6, with sports writers in the papers writing how Washington needs to fire their coach. Tonight Washington was thirty-four point under dogs in Las

Vegas, with nobody giving them a chance of winning tonight's game against Dallas.

"Oh, do you follow football?" I heard her ask me. "Do you like the Redskins, too? I know Washington will win tonight," she continued on. "I think their quarterback is so cute, don't you agree?" She was looking at me like we were finally making a connection and she might like me after all. A bell went off in my brain, and I could tell by the tone in her voice and the way she was looking at me this was the moment that if I ever thought anything could happen with me and her, the correct answer was I love those Redskins...But like my mother always said, I was passed over when they were passing out brains on how to deal with females. Hell, even Lillie, my female golden retriever, keeps running away from me unless I feed her or rub her belly.

I stood there thinking of what I should say to make this right.

She noticed my hesitation, and before I could think of a way out of this trap, she turned her car off and jumped out and stood looking at me in disbelief and yelled, "Don't tell me you're a Cowboys fan," like she was going to challenge me to a fight. Just at that moment, when she got in my face and challenged me, it was as if God was on her side and agreed with her because a big crack of lighting lit up the skies and it started to rain again.

Looking at her now, I could see little beads of rain in her hair and on her face, and this strong, determined look that she wanted to kick my behind because I liked the Dallas Cowboys. I stood there thinking she was the most beautiful girl I've ever seen, even though she was a Washington Redskins fan.

I was thinking if I told her that I really didn't like the Redskins, I was sure that would be strike three with her, and she would drive away and never speak to me again. I just stood there not knowing what to say. I was always told, silence is golden. Then she started laughing.

She told me she was just pulling my leg. She knew I was a huge Cowboys fan because she has seen all the posters and pictures of the players and team pictures on my office walls. It took me awhile to realize how scared and unsure of myself she just made me feel. She played me, making me act like a high school kid.

As I was watching her laugh, she grabbed my hand and said, "You're too easy, Ryan Carter, I'm going to have fun with you," and she leaned up and gave me a kiss.

I just stood there, like I was frozen to the ground, asking myself what the hell just happened? The next thing I knew, I was laughing harder than I've laughed in years. We were both in the middle of the parking lot, standing in almost ankle-deep water, laughing like kids. I didn't care if anyone saw us. I hadn't felt this alive in years. She told me she knew nothing about football, but because she knew I was a Cowboy's fan, she wanted to give me a hard time by wearing a Washington Redskins sweatshirt. I invited her to have some pizza and to watch the game with me, but she wanted to get home and prep for tomorrow's interviews. She jumped back into her car and started it up again, I was hating to see her go. I heard the roar from the muffler and saw the big cloud of black smoke, and for a second, I got excited as I watched her roll her window down, hoping she changed her mind about the pizza. Only to hear her ask if I could push her car out of the parking space because the car didn't have reverse.

After I pushed the car out and with it facing in the right direction, she drove away and yelled, "See you tomorrow, Ryan Carter." I was still laughing as I watched her drive out of the parking lot and turn left onto Arizona Avenue, still hearing the sound from the muffler as she got onto Interstate 85. Now standing there, I noticed I was soaking wet, I didn't care. Picking up my taco pizza at Hector's Pizza Emporium, I raced home to watch the game.

Sitting on the couch, I was thinking life was good. I was watching a Cowboys football game, eating a taco pizza, and remembering the laughs I just had with Kathleen McDonald. Even Lillie seemed to enjoy the night as I scratched her belly. Three hours later, I woke up on the couch; I had fallen asleep and missed the game. Lillie was gone, and I could see the local El Paso channel 7 midnight news on the television. The big story was the Cowboys lost to the Redskins 27 to 7. Ouch.

Chapter Seven
Friday, July 24th, 1993

By pulling into the parking lot at 6:30 the next morning gave me a front row and close to the front door parking space. More rain was in the forecast today, and I didn't want to swim to my car again. As I was being patted down and scanned by security, I had to listen to them complain about last night's game; the consensus was that the referees made bad calls and caused the Cowboys to lose. I took the elevator up to the sixth floor and was surprised to see both LaPinta and McDonald already sitting at the conference table with stacks of paper in front of them. Both of them deeply entrenched in reading their notes for today's interviews. LaPinta looked up and said good morning while ADA McDonald never looked up and continued to read. There was a part of me hoping she would have stood up and give me a kiss good morning. But that didn't happen. Only in my dreams. At least she wasn't wearing her Washington Redskins sweatshirt.

I walked to the end of the conference table and sat down at what has been assigned as my chair. I felt a little unprepared for all I had was a blank tablet of paper and pen in front of me while they all had stacks of folders and boxes in front of them. The conference room door opened, and in walked Deputy Director Galone. We all said our good mornings again and thankfully nobody mentioned last night's game.

I went over all of our planned interviews of Betty Lou and George Quantel, Sheriff Simons, and Barry Richards with everyone. To my surprise, both LaPinta and McDonald requested we have all four sitting at the table at the same time while we ask them questions. The conference room door opened again, and in walked a court appointed stenographer to take notes of today's interviews. She set her table behind me and off to the side and sat waiting for the interviews to begin. As we were all doing our thing to get set up for today's interviews, the telephone on the table rang. We all looked at it wondering who could be calling this room. It kept ringing...one ring...two rings...three rings...each ring sounding a little louder than the one before, as if someone was saying pick up the phone. Still no one was willing to answer it. We all just sat and looked at the phone. After the fourth ring, it finally stopped. The room got deadly silent. Now we all looked at each other thinking of why nobody got up and answered the phone.

With LaPinta finally saying, "I hope we didn't miss an important call." We all gave out a slight laugh and went back to work. Well we didn't have to wait long to find out. The phone started ringing again.

This time, because I'm the mature one, I got up and reached for the phone, saying to nobody in particular but loud enough for everyone to hear, "I bet it's the donut guy saying he's bringing them up with the coffee."

As I answered it, the security guard downstairs told me there was a Barry Richards and Betty Lou and George Quantel with their attorney at the security desk saying they have an 8:00 appointment in the conference room. He was wondering if he should send them up. I told him we were expecting them and to send them up and for him to come up also and told him to plan on staying as security for up to four hours during our interview. When I hung up, everyone was looking at me wondering who was on the phone. I said it was security and he's bringing the donuts and coffee up.

Everyone got excited, even Ms. McDonald started clearing the table for space for the donuts. Now feeling guilty at my attempt at being funny, I had to say, "Just kidding." No one laughed. I did notice a smile from the stenographer though. I informed everyone that our interviews would be starting in about ten minutes, security is bringing them up now. Deputy Director gave me a glare; I think he was upset that there would be no donuts. So far I had not heard from Sheriff Simons. So I picked up the phone and called down to the Sheriff's office and was told he had not come in yet. I left a message for him to call me. We all heard the commotion of everyone getting off the elevator and them walking down the hallway. The door opened, and they all walked in and stopped and took in the imposing view of the room. I gave them a second to look everything over. Then I walked over and introduced myself and asked them to take a chair at the table. I noticed Betty Lou didn't look at me.

The security guard pulled a chair over by the door and sat down. After everyone sat down, I gave them a couple of moments to compose themselves. I stood up and asked if we could go around the table with each of us to say and spell our names for the stenographer to have in her report.

"George Quantel, Betty Lou Quantel, Peter Fedorov, attorney for the Quantel's, Barry Richards, representing myself." Each looking at the stenographer as they spoke and spelling their names.

I spoke up then and said, "And representing the government in this procedure, I will read and spell their names. Edward LaPinta, John Galone, Kathleen McDonald, and myself, Ryan Carter." After that was completed, I looked at the stenographer to make sure she had what she needed, and looking at the clock, which now said 8:20,

I pointed to the empty chair and said that we were still waiting for Sheriff Simons. "We will move ahead and still start the interviews. I'm sure he will show up shortly." But in the back of my mind, I was thinking this was not like Sheriff Simons, he was always punctual.

Deputy Director Galone started off by saying, "This is an informational interview with transcripts of the interview to be sent to the Department of Justice for their review. The scope of this interview will include the murders of John and Harriet Colver. The arrest and execution of Howard Mitchel and the murders of six of the jurors named Kenneth Wilson, Joseph Tate, Doris Harper, Howard Baker, James Devale, and Donald Lampley and the murder of lead prosecutor, Vernon Birchmeyer."

George Quantel jumped up from his chair, and in a stern and loud voice, said, "We have nothing to do with any of these deaths." He turned to his wife, Betty Lou, and said, "Let's go, we're leaving."

As they hurriedly walked towards the door, Deputy Director Galone started shifting through some papers stacked in front of him; as he produced the page he was looking for, he stood up and said to them, "You have the right to leave this room, and as I said, this is an informal interview, but I want to tell you that once you leave this room, you will be arrested and charged with nine counts of premeditated murder, five counts as co-conspirators of drug smuggling, falsifying documents for the jury selection for the trial of Howard Mitchel, and that's just the start. I am handing documents of criminal charges we plan on taking to the Grand Jury to your attorney now for him to review. I promise you that you will not make it to the elevator before I have handcuffs on both of you." With the security guard standing and blocking the door, they both stopped.

George slowly turned around to face us. His face was red, and I could see his eyes were watering up. He took a large, deep breath and let it out slowly. We all, including George, could hear the light sobs of crying coming from Betty Lou as she stood next to him. She still had her back to us, and I could see light tremors of her body shaking. I wanted in the worst way to run up and give her a big hug. But I just sat there. Believing none of this was happening, George put his arm around her shoulders and held her. She turned slowly, and they both walked back to their chairs, Betty Lou never looking up. With Betty Lou now sitting in her chair and George still standing next to her, he looked straight at me with his head shaking up and down, like he was saying yes. I could tell he was thinking of what he wanted to say. His attorney, Peter Fedorov, walked up and stood next to him and whispered something to him, but George brushed him off and said this has been nagging at both of them for almost twenty years.

"We got in over our heads," he said calmly, almost in a whisper. "I should say we got in over our heads because of me. I started drinking and gambling, and it got out of control. The next thing I knew, we didn't have any money. The bank was going to take our house from us, and Betty Lou was talking about leaving me." He took a deep breath, looked at Betty Lou, and said, "I'm so sorry, honey, I didn't mean for any of this to happen." I noticed Betty Lou did not acknowledge or look at him. She just sat there and looked at her hands, still sobbing.

George gave a slight cough, cleared his throat, and he continued, "Sheriff Simons came out to our house one night and said he could help. He knew of our problems," he said. "Betty Lou told him about my drinking and gambling and our money problems. The Sheriff said he wanted to help and said he had a guy who helped him when his wife was dying of cancer and he was short of cash. The medical bills for his wife broke him," he said. "He already had sold his house to pay towards some of the hospital and doctor bills.

The Sheriff told us he had to sell everything, including cashing out his retirement fund, but all that still wasn't enough. He still had bill collectors calling him and coming to his house. Sheriff Simons told us how he finally had to borrow $10,000 from this guy, but the deal was he had to pay him $15,000 back in sixty days, or it would be $3,000 interest per day if he was late. He was kind of like a loan shark, the Sheriff said, definitely not the normal person you wanted to be borrowing money from, but when the bank cuts you off, you don't have much of a choice.

So the Sheriff set it up for us to meet this guy. He seemed nice and sounded like he was concerned and really wanted to help us. So we borrowed the $10,000 from this guy," George continued. "He gave us the same deal as he gave the Sheriff. We were to pay him $15,000 back in sixty days, or it would be $3,000 per day interest." George looked at all of us with a defeated look on his face and said, "I really thought I could pay it off within the sixty days. His name was Alexander Romancoff."

"We sold everything we had left, we even cashed in the balance of both of our retirement plans. I already had taken some money out of the accounts before to pay off some bills, but I was still a little over $2,000 short."

I jumped up and yelled, "You did have a choice, why didn't you ask me? I would have given you the money."

George looked at me and said, "Betty Lou would not let me ask you." I sat back down into my chair, sick to my stomach. Why didn't I see this happening to my friends, or even yet, why didn't they call me? I kept going over and over in my head these questions. After a minute, I motioned for George to continue.

"Romancoff would not give me a break," George said. "He kept telling me I was short some $2,000. He said the deal was for me to give him $15,000, and if he didn't have that by the end of the day, he was going to charge me the additional $3,000 interest per day that we agreed on." George said he left Romancoff's office scared and not knowing what to do. He tried to avoid Romancoff, but it seemed like George was always seeing him in town. At the grocery store, at the gas station, Romancoff even drove by where George worked.

George continued to say with a defeated tone, "As I look back at it now, I'm sure he was following me."

George told us that after a week or so went by, Romancoff was at the front door of their home.

"Romanoff didn't say anything, he and his three goons just walked up, grabbed me, and beat and kicked the hell out of me. Romancoff said he would be back in two days for his money, or he would come back and start breaking bones." I started to stand up, but George stopped me with a wave of his hand and said there's more.

As I sat back down, George continued by saying, "A week later, Romancoff and his three goons stopped me on my way home from work. They forced me into their car and took me to the house of Mr. Michael Mancini. He's the owner of the company I work for, All Safe Security Company," George said. George then looked and pointed at Barry Richards, the attorney, and said, "He was there also."

I looked at Deputy Director Galone and said, "Now that's interesting that Mancini and Romancoff know each other," and as I pointed to Richards, I said, "And Mr. Richards, I think you're about to be busy with the District Attorney's office." Richards didn't say anything, he just stared at George.

We all listened as George spoke up again and said, "Romancoff and Mancini not only know each other, they're in business together. Mancini seems to be the boss of everything." I could tell George was on a roll with information.

Mancini told George that because he's been a good employee, he wanted to help George with his problem with Romancoff. George was told that if he looked the other way on the deliveries of drugs to the incinerator at Laughlin Air Force Base, Mancini would not only take care of George's debt that he owed Romancoff, but Mancini would also give George $1,000 for each trip Apache Transport made to the incinerator.

"All I had to do was sign the delivery papers and not ask questions," George said. "I thought what was bad about that," he said with a smile on his face and looking at everyone. "I never told Betty Lou what the arrangement was, I just told her I took care of everything," George continued by saying that he overheard Romancoff make a statement to Mancini that they will now have the Sheriff on the front end and I would be on the back end of each load of drugs to the incinerator, what could go wrong, it was perfect," and they both laughed.

I spoke up, then to nobody in general by saying, "They must still have their hooks in the Sheriff if he's feeding them info about each delivery."

I then turned to the security guard by the door and asked him to call down to the sheriff's office again, he is now over an hour late. Find out what's going on. I watched the guard stand up and walk over to the wall telephone and make the call, still dissecting what George just told everyone. It didn't look good for the Sheriff.

LaPinta stood up and looked at me and said, "I think I have more information on this Alexander Romancoff."

I had to put my hand up for him to stop talking because we all hear loud commotion coming from the security guard as he hung up the wall telephone by the door. Everyone in the room was looking and watching him, wondering what was going on.

He was only about fifteen feet away from us, but he felt it was necessary for him to run towards us and stop about two feet from me and yell, "They just found Sheriff Simons two miles north of town in his squad car. Dead. Shot in the head. The County's full investigation team is on the way there now." You could tell this was the most excitement he has ever had as a security guard, as he was talking very fast and moving around like his shoes were on fire.

Betty Lou gave out a horrifying scream. George kept saying, "No, no, no...this can't be happening." We all knew the sheriff was a close friend of theirs. I jumped up and said we were going to suspend this interview for the day. I turned back to the security guard and told him to calm down and to take Attorney Barry Richards into custody.

Richards jumped up and yelled, "For what? I didn't do anything." I told him he was at most a witness to conspire a drug operation between Mancini and Romancoff. I reached for the telephone on the desk and called down for sheriff's deputies to come to this conference room on the double. I turned to ADA McDonald and told her I wanted arrest warrants issued for both Michael Mancini and Alexander Romancoff ASAP. She yelled back she was on it as she ran out the door.

Barry Richards was still yelling and making demands to the security guard, I could see the guard was struggling with him, so I walked over, grabbed Richards by the back of his neck, and pushed him into the wall. I then put the handcuffs on him and forced him to sit in his chair. He looked at me and gave me a grin and said how about making a bet that he'll be back out on the street in less than five hours...I told him if I were a betting man, I would take that bet, but I think your golden goose has flown the coop.

Just then four deputies walked into the room. They took Richards into custody without any more problems. I also instructed them to hold and put into police protection George and Betty Lou Quantel. The four deputies all knew Betty Lou, but I still pointed out to them to make sure, and said under no condition are they to leave this building. I looked at both George and Betty Lou, neither said anything.

I walked over to them; they both stood up, and we did a three-person hug. We all cried. They agreed about the police protection. I told them Agent LaPinta of the FBI would be talking to them. The deputies, along with Agent LaPinta, walked them out of the room. ADA McDonald came back into the room then, and she and Deputy Director Galone stood next to me.

"Arrest warrants had been issued for both Mancini and Romancoff," she said. I felt totally exhausted. My head was buzzing with questions on with this whole case.

I heard myself say, "Thank you. Good job," as I watched George and Betty Lou be escorted out the room.

Deputy Director Galone nudged me and asked me what the next step is. I told him about my plans to see the Judge tomorrow. He started walking towards the door, told me I should go home and rest. We've all had a very busy and exciting day. He said he would keep me posted with any updates about the sheriff.

Kathleen McDonald looked at me and said, "Are all your days like this?" I was thinking about the death of Sheriff Simons and the story George Quantel just told us. I know I could have helped them both. This did not have to happen, I was telling myself.

I could feel tears filling up in my eyes, tears of sadness and anger. I had to turn away from her because I didn't want her to see me almost crying.

I started walking towards the door, saying to her, "Let's meet here tomorrow morning at 8:00, so we can go meet the Judge." Not waiting for her reply, I just walked out the door and almost ran to the elevators, but I realized I needed to walk some to clear my head, so I took the stairs down the three flights of stairs to the third floor where my office is. I just kept re-thinking this whole case. The arrest and conviction of Howard Mitchel, George Quantel, and the incinerator, the crimes of Mancini and Romancoff and now the death of the Sheriff. I was telling myself that there's still more to come, and I haven't reached the end of the story yet.

I was in such deep thought about this case that the next thing I knew I was on the ground floor. I had walked down the six flights of stairs and now stood in the courthouse lobby. I really didn't want to go to my office anyways, so I started walking towards the front door and went home. I didn't even notice all the commotion in the lobby with the press setting up their cameras so they could get the latest scoop about Sheriff Simons. That night I hardly slept. My mind wouldn't turn off. I know my telephone rang a number of times. I never answered it.

Chapter Eight
Saturday, July 25th, 1993

Being 8:00 A.M. on a Saturday morning, the court house parking lot was almost empty. Except for the activity from the sheriff's department and television vans, no one else was working, so parking was not a problem. After going through the security maze, I went straight up to the sixth floor where Kathleen McDonald and Edward LaPinta were already sitting waiting for me. The first thing I noticed was a coffee pot and plate of donuts on the table, compliments of the District Attorney's Office McDonald said. With the three of us eating a donut and drinking a cup of coffee, we went over yesterday's interview. I told them both how I couldn't sleep last night. How I kind of blame myself for not being aware of the Quantels and the Sheriff's problems. I know I could have helped them. Both agreed I should not blame myself. We all agreed that yesterday was more explosive than was expected. LaPinta said that putting George and Betty Lou in protective custody was a good thing.

McDonald saying, "George's testimony will be vital to the case."

With my mouth full of a donut but still trying to act professionally, I tried to say, "If we know that, so do Mancini and Romancoff, so we have to make sure George and Betty Lou stay safe." I asked if there was any word on the arrest warrants on Mancini and Romancoff.

McDonald said she checked, and deputies had been to both of their houses and offices and there was no sign of them. We have deputies stationed at all locations in case they show up.

"I'm thinking we might have to squeeze Richards," LaPinta said. "He's such a weasel. I think if we offer him a deal, he will tell us everything we want to know, including where Mancini and Romancoff might be now."

Taking my last gulp of coffee, I said, "That's a great idea, do you want to talk to Richards today or let him sit for the weekend?"

"Let's let him sit for the weekend," LaPinta said. "Let's see what the arrest warrants turn up. A man like Richards is not use to sitting in jail, so the longer he sits behind bars, the more eager he'll be to talk to us later."

"Okay then," I said, "let's plan our interview with the Judge then." As if on cue, Deputy Director Galone walked in, and spotting the coffee and donuts on the table, smiled and said nice touch.

He poured himself a cup of coffee and said, "I think we should all go together to interview the Judge. I don't know if you all know this, but I was in Albert Rivera's wedding thirty years ago." The Director said this while looking at us but also looking at the last donut in the box. I don't think he really was expecting us to engage into a conversation with him on the Judge's wedding, he was more like making a statement.

"Must be thirty years ago now since I've seen him. It will be nice to see him again," he said as he grabbed the last donut and started walking out of the room. "I'll meet you by the front door in say thirty minutes," he yelled, "and I think we should have LaPinta drive, I've seen how you drive Ryan, and it scares me." We all sat there and watched the door close after him. It was the first time that I could remember that I saw a friendly side of the Director." We all burst out laughing at the same time, finding it interesting that we might hear stories of the Director when he was younger. Except for the almost three-hour drive ahead of us to Dell City where the Judge now lives, I was hoping it would be a good day and we would get answers about the Howard Mitchel case.

We all climbed into an FBI unmarked Chevy Suburban, with La-Pinta driving and the Director riding shotgun in the front and me sitting in the back seat next to Kathleen McDonald. It was a warm, sunny day, and with me not sleeping at all last night, I'm sure I fell asleep before we got out of the parking lot.

The next thing I remember, I woke up with my head on Kathleen's shoulder. It seemed like we just got into the car, but my watch told me we had been driving for almost three hours.

I sat up and apologized for falling asleep. LaPinta yelled out we will be there in about ten minutes. I was feeling a little groggy from my deep sleep, and I needed to clear my head before we met with the Judge and I said as much to everyone. Kathleen said her mother had a way of waking he father up from a deep sleep. I said and how was that? She turned to me, and I have to admit, I thought she was going to give me a kiss to perk me up, but instead she hauled off and slapped me in my face.

"What the hell was that for?" I yelled.

She came back with, "My mother said it works every time."

As I sat there rubbing my face, I heard the Director say to La-Pinta, "They make a lovely couple, don't you think?" And I heard one of his rare laughs. I have to admit, I didn't feel groggy anymore.

Driving up to the house and after stretching our legs and spending about thirty minutes with our introductions and listening to the Director and the Judge go down memory lane, we were finally sitting on the back patio drinking some iced tea and were ready to start the interview. The Judge started by saying he was expecting us and he was excited to see us so quickly.

"Why just yesterday afternoon, Sheriff Simons said he was going to talk to you and set up this meeting." I asked the Judge what it was he and the Sheriff talked about yesterday. The Judges response kind of surprised me. "Why, we talked about the Howard Mitchel case of course," he said. "But you already know that," he said with a strange look on his face. The Judge continued by saying, "Sheriff Simons came out here and told me you were looking at some old cases, particularly the Howard Mitchel case." Looking at us with a grin on his face, he continued, "As you know, I'm very familiar with that case." The way he was looking at us and the way he was talking to us just now got my blood to boil a little, it was like he was taunting us.

Kathleen McDonald must have picked up on that attitude also and spoke with a little anger in her voice, "Sir, we're out here to get information from you on that case. And I'm not sure you realize it, but most legal scholars say there were many errors and a huge injustice to the defendant. You yourself were censored by the Texas Legal and Ethical board for the way you handled the case. All the evidence we've uncovered shows Howard Mitchel did not and could not have committed those murders. And I'm pretty sure you knew that at the trial. And yet you still sentenced him and refused his six appeals. You, sir, in effect killed an innocent man." The room got quiet. I have to give Kathleen credit, she got in his face with her remarks. And she was still looking at the Judge with a totally disrespectful look. She was not backing down at all. The Judge gave Kathleen a look of anger. At first a very mean and stern look like he was saying how dare you talk to me like that. I'm sure he was not used to anyone, especially a woman, talking to him like that and especially not in that tone.

Being raised by the old-fashioned good old boys club, I'm sure the Judge was taught that all women were to know their place in society and were to just say yes, sir, and no, sir, especially when they were talking to a man. Well, I said to myself, he was talking to the wrong woman about that attitude today. But the Judges tone softened as he looked at McDonald and he hesitated to say any harsh words that he could not take back.

While looking at her like a father would look at his daughter after she broke his heart with harsh words, he said in a much calmer tone, "You don't mind if I call you Kathleen, do you?" But before she could answer, he said, "Kathleen, you are absolutely correct. And I would be a devil of man if I didn't feel some remorse, but Sheriff Simons and I didn't have a choice back then."

The judge got up and offered to refill our glasses of iced tea. Letting his last statement sink in before he continued.

As he returned to his chair, he said, "Yesterday Sheriff Simons and I agreed it was time for us to tell the truth. The Sheriff said he was going to make an appointment with you all." That's why you're here, because he called you, right?"

"Sir," I said, "we're here because of our investigation. Sheriff Simons never contacted us. As a matter of fact, I'm sorry to say Sheriff Simons was found murdered yesterday, probably on his way from leaving here." The Judge dropped his glass of tea in total shock and just looked at us.

The Judge jumped up from his chair and started pacing around the patio. "What happened?" he said. Shaking his arms and talking in a high terror-stricken tone.

"We don't have all the answers at this moment," I said. "He was found shot to death in his car a couple of miles from the courthouse. Presumably after he left here and was probably on his way to talk to us." That got the Judge all worked up, his smug and taunting attitude now gone and a more scared attitude was on full display.

"Why don't you start from the beginning and tell us everything you know?" I said.

In a hysterical tone, the Judge said, "I will need protection; if he could get to Sheriff Simons, he can get to me also."

I stood up and walked over to the Judge, taking him by his arm and sitting him down in his chair.

"We will call and have deputies stationed outside. So Judge, please tell me, from the beginning, what you know about the Howard Mitchel case," I said.

The Judge looked at me with total fear in his eyes and said, "Vernon Birchmeyer and his big shot friend Michael Mancini threatened to kill my wife and Sheriff Simons' wife if we didn't do as we were told." The Judge then told us a story that left all of us glued to our chairs listening. "It all had to do with a large shipment of cocaine that was coming from Mexico and was to be delivered to a house in Fort Stockton," he started. "I think the last name of the home owner was Cruz, Louis Cruz or something like that," the Judge said, trying to get a memory recall from his brain.

"This Cruz guy worked for Mancini, he was going to be the main drug dealer in the area for Mancini. Anyways the whole deal went bad." The Judge, running his hands through his hair, said, "Mancini made arrangements to have one of his goons drop off a package of money at the Cruz's house to pay for the large shipment of cocaine that was coming from Mexico. Mancini sent his goon to the address Birchmeyer gave him, which turned out was the wrong address. The address he was given was John and Harriet Colver's address. With a stranger pounding at their door in the middle of the night, the Colver's got scare and threatened to call the cops if he didn't leave.

So Mancini's goon high tailed it out of there, but he still threw the package of cash into the garage attic without John Colver seeing him do that. Mancini was told all of this and still went ahead and told the people in Mexico to drop the cocaine at Louis Cruz's house. Mancini thought he would just go to the Colver's house and retrieve the cash."

The Judge told us, "When Mancini and Birchmeyer went to the Colver's garage, the package of cash wasn't there. They tore the garage apart looking for it but didn't find it. They even dragged the goon out of his home to bring him to the Colver's garage to show Mancini where he put the package. That's when Mancini went crazy and went inside the house and started to torture the Colver's. Trying to find out where the cash was. Mancini knows you don't play games with any Mexican drug dealer when it comes to money. Mancini blamed Birchmeyer for this screw up. I wouldn't be surprised if Mancini didn't order the hit on Birchmeyer," the Judge said.

"If the Colver's didn't take the cash, then someone else did," I said to no one in particular.

The Judge continued by saying, "He was told that Birchmeyer's thinking was with the Colver's being killed from the beatings from Mancini, he didn't want the murders to be tied to any kind of a drug deal. He didn't want the press or the cops thinking there was any kind of drug operation in the area, so he came up with the idea to blame a black man of committing a simple break in or robbery that went bad. Howard Mitchel was always just a diversion. Don't you see, these were some very bad people. The Sheriff and I didn't have a choice. They threatened to kill our families." The Judge, almost yelling this to us, trying to tell us he didn't have a choice and he did the right thing, which made me sick to my stomach.

"Anyways," the Judge said, calming down some, "I guess Mancini never did find the package of cash, and my career in the legal profession as either a Judge or attorney pretty much ended with that case," as he walked back to his chair and sat down.

I looked at the Judge and asked him, "Why were the six jurors hand-picked for the trial?"

"That was Birchmeyer's ideal also. He wanted six jurors that he paid for, that would vote to convict Howard Mitchel because he knew the evidence was not strong enough to get a legal conviction against Howard Mitchel. Like I said, he wanted the case to be all about a robbery or break in gone bad."

The Judge continued with, "Birchmeyer even forged Betty Lou's signature on the jury request form," the Judge said. "I don't think she was aware of the form until you opened the case, I know she talked to Sheriff Simons about it and she was mad as hell, but the Sheriff told her it would be best if she didn't do anything. The Sheriff said he would make sure nothing happened to her."

I looked over at Kathleen and saw she was still looking at the Judge with contempt. The Director was just standing by the patio door listening. We all heard the sound of a car driving up to the house.

LaPinta stood up and said, "That must be the Deputies, I'll go meet them."

I stood up and walked over to the Judge, who now leaned back in his chair and said to me, "I hope you get this Mancini son of a bitch, he did some terrible things."

As LaPinta and the two deputies walked out on the patio and stopped, I said to the Judge, "Yes, Mancini did some terrible things, but so did you. I'm placing you under arrest for the murder of Howard Mitchel."

"You can't arrest me, I'm a Judge," he said.

"Yes, you are a Judge," I said, "and that's the sad thing about this, you used your position to falsely convict a man of a crime he didn't do."

I turned to the deputies and said, "Place this man under arrest and take him back to the El Paso County jail. We will follow you in our car and we will do all the necessary paper work when we get there."

The Judge was mad as hell. He yelled at the Director about their friendship, then looked at me and said he would ruin my career.

I stood in front of the Judge and said, "Maybe you're right, maybe I should just leave you here and I could call Mancini, I'm sure he would know what to do with you." That calmed the Judge down. He almost ran to the squad car. We all walked out to our cars for our long drive back. Nervously I climbed in the back seat with Kathleen and told her I wouldn't fall asleep this time, and she said that's too bad, she was liking the ideal of slapping me again. We all laughed as we drove away. When we got back to the courthouse, we found it pretty quiet. The press vehicles had been moved to the far end of the parking lot. I inquired about the status of Sheriff Simons and was told nothing new yet. No clear evidence of what happened yet we were told. I escorted the Judge into booking, I could see the desk sergeant was kind of nervous with the paper work. It's not every day you book a U.S. District Judge in for murder, I said to myself. We now had the Judge, George, and Betty Lou and the sleazy attorney Barry Richards all locked up. I told Kathleen and LaPinta that Monday we would put the screws to Barry Richards as to where we can find Mancini and Romancoff.

I said to everyone, "Let's take tomorrow off and hit it hard on Monday." I heard no complaints.

Chapter Nine
Monday, July 27th, 1993

This morning I was awake, showered, and dressed by 3:30 A.M. I've never been so eager to get to work. I thought yesterday could not go any slower. I didn't even watch a football game. I just kept reading and re-reading my notes from this case. I drove into the parking lot at 6:00 A.M., which gave me a good parking spot. While going through security without too much problem, I was told nothing new on Sheriff Simons shooting. I walked down to the county jail to check in with Betty Lou and George. They were both happy to see me. They asked how the case was going. I told them about the Judge. They were surprised to hear he was in jail. We talked about Barry Richards, and I told them how I'm hoping he would know where Mancini and Romancoff were. I told both of them to be patient and I would keep in touch.

Taking the elevator up to the sixth floor gave me time to make my plan for Barry Richards. The sad thing was I still didn't have a plan. For the first time since this case began, I was the first person in the conference room. After turning on all the lights and getting my notes spread out in front of me, I picked up the phone and called down to the jail and instructed them to bring inmate Barry Richards up to the sixth floor conference room at 8:00.

Both LaPinta and McDonald walked into the room a little before 8:00. I brought them up to speed with updates on Sheriff Simons and me seeing Betty Lou and George and with having Barry Richards brought up here in about ten minutes. The conference room door opened, and thinking it would be Barry Richards, we were surprised to see Deputy Galone instead. As he walked in, he was eying the table, and I saw the slight disappointment of no coffee and donuts, but being a good trooper that he is, he didn't say anything and just sat down and asked where we were at with today's interview.

Before I could answer, two deputies escorted Barry Richards into the room and handcuffed him to the chair across from me. I could tell Richards was mad. I asked him if he liked his orange jumpsuit and handcuffs. At first it looked like he wasn't going to say anything...but then he exploded...he started yelling how he wanted his lawyer here before he talks.

"My lawyer and I talked over the weekend, and he's ready to press charges of false imprisonment, and that's just for starters," he said.

"Good luck with that," I said. "Now stop wasting my time and just shut up and listen, I have a deal for you." But Barry Richards must have thought he was holding all the cards because he kept right on yelling that he was not going to say anything without his lawyer here and demanded his right to make his phone call to have his lawyer present.

"You can't interrogate me without my lawyer present," he yelled.

"You're correct, Barry," I said, "we will give you your five minutes of private time to make your phone call." I waved for the deputy to come over to take the handcuffs off Barry so he could make his telephone call, and as I pushed the telephone over, I also set the business card of Clayton Armstrong in front of him.

"When you talk to your lawyer, make sure you tell him the name on this card. Make sure your lawyer knows he will be defending this case against Clayton Armstrong." We all got up from the table and walked out of the room. "See you in five," I said to Richards. As we stood in the hallway, McDonald asked what our plan was. "I really don't have one," I said. "I'm playing this as if we were in a football game, and it's fourth down with two seconds left on the clock. We're throwing a hail Mary pass to the end zone and hope for the best."

She gave me a look of astonishment. "You're throwing football terminology at me for your strategy after all this hard work, and it might all be for nothing because this idiot Barry Richards won't talk," she said, waving her arms and walking in a circle around me. "To have any case against Mancini and Romancoff, we need both the Judge and Richards to testify," LaPinta said.

I looked at both of them and said, "I know, I'm just hoping Richards' lawyer is smarter than Richards is, and he'll want nothing to do with this case or Barry Richards."

LaPinta looked at me and said, "That's a lot to hope for."

Five minutes later, we walked back into the room; I could see Barry was not on the telephone, with his hands now handcuffed again to his chair, he was just sitting looking at the floor.

"How soon can your lawyer be here?" I asked as I slid into my chair. I was thinking I already knew the answer. Barry's visual attitude had changed. He was not the cocky, demanding prick of five minutes ago.

"My lawyer said it would be a waste of his time to come here," Barry said with anger that was directed not at me but at his lawyer. "My former lawyer," Barry spit out, "said no attorney with their right mind would go against Clayton Armstrong. He said I should accept any deal you're offering and run with it."

Leaning back in my chair and giving both LaPinta and McDonald a quick look, I said, "Barry, you have, or should I say you had, a smart lawyer. So let's see if you're as smart as him." I got out of my chair and walked around the table and sat in the chair that was next to him. I gave him a slight pat on his back and said, "Here's the deal I'm giving you. You tell me where Mancini and Romancoff are right now, so we can arrest them and get them off the streets. And you agree to testify about everything you know about their drug operation, up to and including buying drugs from Mexico and rigging the delivery sheets to the incinerator at Laughlin Air Force Base and you clear up George Quantel and the Sheriff. You do all that, Barry, and I guarantee you won't spend any time in jail. You will lose your law license though. Otherwise, Barry, if you don't agree to these terms, I guarantee you that you will spend the rest of your life in prison, and you will still have to deal with Mancini." Barry must have taken his smart pills today because he didn't even hesitate. He did say he wanted some kind of protection.

"Mancini is someone you don't fool around with," he said, knowing the great danger he was putting himself into if he accepted this deal. LaPinta spoke up and told Barry he would be eligible for the witness protection plan, which seemed to motivate Barry's thinking.

Chapter Ten

I will tell you all now that Barry Richards was a man of his word. That night we arrested both Mancini and Romancoff. And to use the phrase "He sang like a canary" would be saying it lightly. Barry Richards gave us information on events we didn't even know about. Like Alexander Romancoff's real name was Petre Navitscof. As in the Petre Navitscof that Clayton Armstrong and the Department of Justice filed extradition papers on. Evidently Petre Navitscof is wanted, specifically in the state of New York, where he was suspected of being the leader of a Russian drug's and firearms operation. The body of Nedia Petrov, the other name on the extradition papers, was found murdered in a burnt-out car five months ago. The body was just identified. The FBI office in New York say that Navitscof has not been seen for over a year, and they speculated that maybe he was dead also, but latest Intel was saying he was suspected to be living in the El Paso area. After the trial here in El Paso, Romancoff, aka Navitscof, was taken into custody by FBI agents from the State of New York and transported there to stand trial for outstanding charges.

It took a couple of months for the Mancini and Romancoff's trial to get started. Clayton Armstrong and U.S. Assistant Attorney General Simon Friedman brought a boat load of top-notch attorneys down to El Paso and got the ball rolling. At the trial, both Judge Rivera and Barry Richards testified against Mancini and Romancoff about the murder of John and Harriet Colver, the framing of Howard Mitchel, the drug operation, and the murder of Vernon Birchmeyer. With their testimony, we put Mancini and Romancoff away for forty years for each count. With Romancoff still having to deal with charges in the State of New York, he is currently trying to work out a deal with New York's Attorney General with information he has on Sheriff Simons' murder.

Barry Richards has been processed into the Witness Protection Program, and his case handler says he is doing just fine. He has taken classes for cooking and is now working as a cook in a location that I'm not allowed to know.

George Quantel lost his job of course. With Mancini going to prison, the company folded and went out of business. The court found George guilty on a reduced charge of falsifying federal documents, and because of his testimony, placed him on probation for five years, and if he keeps himself clean during that time, his record would be cleared.

Betty Lou Quantel retired from the Sheriff's Department. She faced no criminal charges. She and George, with a loan from me, purchased a ten-acre ranch by Midland, Texas and are enjoying their newfound life.

Judge Alberto Rivera refused to accept any plea deal for his testimony against Mancini and Romancoff, he said it was the right thing to do. The courts found Judge Rivera guilty of falsifying court documents and creating false information in the Howard Mitchel murder case, but because of his testimony in the Mancini and Romancoff case and his age, he was eighty-eight-years-old, he was just given a two-year suspended sentenced, his law license was suspended, and he had to pay some financial restitution to the court. He is now living somewhere up by Carson, Nevada the last I heard.

Special Agent Edward LaPinta was given letters of special commendation for his personnel file from Clayton Armstrong and U.S. Assistant Attorney General Simon Friedman for his leadership and perseverance in this case.

U.S. Marshall Deputy Director John Galone also wrote a letter of praise for a job well done. LaPinta was also given a choice location that he could use to transfer to any FBI field office of his choice. He took a position as Special Agent in Charge in the field office in Lincoln, Nebraska to be close to his mother. That's also where my brother lives, Father James Carter, a Catholic priest and pastor at St Peter's Catholic Church. So I told LaPinta to give my brother a call when he gets settled in. It was hard for me to say good bye to LaPinta, he is one of the good guys. I know he will do well in his new assignment.

U.S. Assistant District Attorney Kathleen McDonald was also given letters of commendation from Clayton Armstrong and U.S. Assistant Attorney General Simon Friedman. Deputy Director John Galone also wrote a letter for her personnel file. Her leadership and legal information were of the highest standards they all said. She was not extended any choice location reassignment, but she was moved from her small office to a larger office with windows overlooking the Rio Grande.

Clayton Armstrong requested we have a ceremony for Althea Jones Mitchel. Howard's wife, and their three children. I watched as Clayton Armstrong gave Althea a package that the FBI found in the attic of the Cruz's garage. I'm thinking it was the missing package of cash for the drug purchase. I saw tears on Clayton's face when he talked to Althea in private after the trial. Clayton always made sure seats were reserved for the family in the courtroom during the trial, so they could hear and see everything. I didn't stick around after the ceremony, so I don't know what was said about me. I packed a bag and told Director Galone I was going to take the rest of my vacation and go to Midland, Texas and spend some time with George and Betty Lou.

And I have to say my relationship with Kathleen McDonald has progressed to the next level. After all this time of working with her, she told me nobody calls her Kathleen, except her father when he's mad at her. Her family and friends call her Mac. So Mac and I have been dating, and it has been a fun-filled experience.

Mac and I finally had our first taco pizza and watched a football game together. She really knows nothing about football, but she's learning. Lillie, my golden retriever, likes Mac more than she likes me. The three of us will sit on the couch together watching the game together. If I get to close to Mac, Lillie gives a little growl, causing Mac and I to laugh.

Life is good in my world.